A NEAPOLITAN FESTA A BALLO
and
SELECTED INSTRUMENTAL ENSEMBLE PIECES

Recent Researches in the Music of the Baroque Era is one of four quarterly series (Middle Ages and Early Renaissance; Renaissance; Baroque Era; Classical Era) which make public the early music that is being brought to light in the course of current musicological research.

Each volume is devoted to works by a single composer or in a single genre of composition, chosen because of their potential interest to scholars and performers, and prepared for publication according to the standards that govern the making of all reliable historical editions.

Correspondence should be addressed:

A-R Editions, Inc.
315 West Gorham Street
Madison, Wisconsin 53703

RECENT RESEARCHES IN THE MUSIC OF THE BAROQUE ERA • VOLUME XXV

A NEAPOLITAN FESTA A BALLO

"Delizie di Posilipo Boscarecce, e Maritime"

and

SELECTED INSTRUMENTAL ENSEMBLE PIECES

from Naples Conservatory MS 4.6.3.

Edited by Roland Jackson

A-R EDITIONS, INC. • MADISON

Per la cara Brenda

"Qual de' vostr'occhi
Feri, o benigni
Spiegano i Cigni
Con dolce canto. . . ."

—No.[9], *Aria de Venere*

Copyright © 1978, A-R Editions, Inc.

ISSN 0484-0828

ISBN 0-89579-093-9

Library of Congress Cataloging in Publication Data:

Delizie di Posilipo boscarecce, e maritime.
    A Neapolitan festa a ballo = Delizie de Posilipo
boscarecce, e maritime, and Selected instrumental
ensemble pieces from Naples Conservatory ms. 4.6.3.

    (Recent researches in the music of the baroque
era ; v. 25 ISSN 0484-0828)
    1. Masques with music — Scores. 2. Dance music.
3. Instrumental music. I. Jackson, Roland,
fl. 1967-   II. Naples. Conservatorio di musica
"San Pietro a Majella." MSS. (4.6.3.) III. Title.
IV. Series.
M2.R238 vol. 25 [M1520] [M1450] 780'.903'2s [782.9]
ISBN 0-89579-093-9   78-14587

Contents

Selected Instrumental Ensemble Pieces
from Naples Conservatory MS 4.6.3.

Preface

The Festa a Ballo
"Delizie di Posilipo Boscarecce, e Maritime"

The Festa a Ballo as a Genre

The *festa a ballo,* as the name implies, was a lavish Italian court festival featuring the dance. As such it formed a parallel in the sixteenth and seventeenth centuries with the *ballet de cour* in France and the masque in England. These spectacles had many features in common; they grew out of the simpler entertainments (such as masks or mummeries) of the early Renaissance, and reached an apex in the elaborate court productions, such as *Circe* (1581) in France or the lavish *intermedii* known as *La Pellegrina* (1589) in Florence. These presentations set a standard in opulence for those that followed during the seventeenth century. Although elements of opera were incorporated into the court entertainments, the two genres remained fundamentally different: opera had a dramatic focus and a continuity in which vocal recitative predominated; the court spectacles depended principally on visual display and the dance, and the vocal numbers that were included did not support a dramatic continuity.

The courtly dance spectacles were similar from one country to another. They began with laudatory musical numbers addressed to a local dignitary, continued with a varied succession of scenes performed by professional dancers and singers, and concluded with a grand dance in which the aristocracy took part. English and French entertainments of this kind have been fairly well documented by scholarly research. However, our knowledge of their counterpart at the Italian courts is limited. A comparative study that examines the various kinds of Italian spectacles *(trionfe, mascherate, feste a ballo,* and, of course, the *intermedii)* and their relationship to those of England and France has not yet been made. Thus, the Neapolitan *festa a ballo* published for the first time in this volume is of special interest: it offers a rare example of an early seventeeth-century Italian dance entertainment. Moreover, this work has been preserved in integral form: that is, with a text and much of the corresponding music.

The Breve Racconto della Festa a Ballo

The Neapolitan *festa a ballo* "Delizie di Posilipo Boscarecce, e Maritime" is preserved in a single source: the *Breve Racconto della Festa a Ballo* ("A Brief Report of the Dance Festival . . .") published in 1620.[1] This source is notable because in addition to the text it includes a substantial part of the original music as well as a number of dance diagrams. Most other court entertainments contemporaneous with the one in the present edition can only be reconstructed from several different sources (for example, by matching the published texts with contemporary collections of vocal pieces).

The contents of the *Breve Racconto della Festa a Ballo* are as follows. Textual section: p. [1]—Title page ("BREVE RACCONTO DELLA FESTA A BALLO"); pp. 3-15—general remarks, stage directions, and a complete libretto. Musical section: p. [1]—Title page ("CANZONETTE RAPPRESENTATE IN MUSICA NELLA DETTA FESTA"); pp. 2-35, music, vocal and instrumental (some instrumental numbers alluded to in the libretto are lacking). Dance section: pp. 1-2—dance formations ("FIGURE DEL BALLO DE CAVALIERI").

The *Breve Racconto* was first brought to scholarly attention in 1894 by N. D'Arienzo,[2] who called it "a cantata with action" and reproduced the "Aria de Venere" by Trabaci and the "Suono del Ballo de Cigni" by Spiardo ([9] and [12] in the present edition). In his observation that the aria anticipated certain of the qualities of later composers such as Cesti, D'Arienzo probably noticed the lilting triple rhythm and the smooth melodic line over a recurrent thorough bass pattern; these features distinguish the "Aria de Venere" from the other pieces in the collection.

Historical Background

The Neapolitan *festa a ballo* in this edition was first presented on Carnival Sunday, March 1, 1620. A reason for these particular festivities, in addition to its being the pre-Lenten time, lay in "the happiness occasioned by the return to health of His Catholic Majesty, Philip III of Austria, King of the Spains"[3] (see Plate I). This reference to Philip could explain the printing (which was unusual for court spectacles) of this *festa.* In any case, Philip's representative, the Viceroy Don Pedro Giron, was present on this occasion and was made the subject of the various laudatory pieces near the beginning of the work (numbers [2], [3], and [5]). Giron's reputation for his sponsorship of court spectacles was such that a Neapolitan court chronicler, writing more than a half century later, still alluded to it:[4] "Crebbe verso del Viceré l'universale benivolenza, per la moltitudine delle feste, conviti, giostre, danze, tornei, ed altri esercizj cavallereschi, che continuamente promoveva, ed ordinava, anche a sue proprie spese, con tanta magnificenze, ch'agguagliava per non dire, che superava quella degli antichi Romani." ("Goodwill toward the viceroy increased in every quarter due to the many festivals, banquets, jousts, dance spectacles, tourneys, and equestrian shows he continually commanded, and sponsored even at his own expense. So magnificent were they, in fact, that they equaled, not to say surpassed, those of the ancient Romans.") Giron's spectacles may have impressed the courtiers at home; but he was deeply embroiled in political intrigue abroad. Things came to a head in 1620, when his secret conspiracy to wrest Naples from Spanish power and become an independent ruler was discovered. Giron was quickly overthrown by a surprise appearance of the Spanish militia in June of 1620; subsequently he was returned to Madrid, where he reportedly died in prison.[5] In light of this, the text of the *festa a ballo* takes on a hollow ring, especially when we hear Giron described as a "Phoebus" in [2] and praised in [3] as follows: "In great GIRON ("GIRO" forms an obvious pun) is united/as in a starry COURSE/ Fame, Time, and Fortune, together with Envy./ These he has as his subjects, and of their power he has no fear."

The Music

The Neapolitan spectacle of this edition belongs to the category of *pasticcio:* it is the result of a collaboration by several composers, including Giovanni Maria Trabaci (the court chapelmaster) and Francesco Lambardi (court organist), as well as Pietro Antonio Giramo (known mainly for his later musical activities in Tuscany), Andrea Ansalone (of a family of local Neapolitan wind performers), and Giacomo Spiardo (the dancing master of the original presentation of this *festa a ballo*). Trabaci and Lambardi composed the important vocal numbers, Giramo the villanella-like opening piece, and Ansalone and Spiardo the instrumental numbers (at least those that are printed in the *Breve Racconto*). Both the music and the composer designations for [6], [8], [10], and [15] are missing in the *Breve Racconto*. Spiardo's "Suono del Ballo de'Selvaggi, e delle Simie" [14] offers an unusual example of instrumental writing: its parallel fifths and awkward leaps indicate the hand of an amateur; however, its bizarre rhythms, apparently inspired by the grotesque movements of this dance, clearly represent an attempt at musical humor.

The instrumental scoring called for in the print differentiated between the various kinds of scene, as had become customary in earlier *intermedii*. The sylvan scenes were associated with wind instruments: shawms *(ciaramelle)* for Pan's entrance; bagpipes *(sordelline)* for his initial dance; and simply wind instruments *(istromenti di fiato)* for the dance of the satyrs and apes. The aristocratic characters were distinguished by the playing of trumpets *(trombe)* to introduce the scene where they form their *cortège* around Venus; and their main dances required an orchestra of forty instruments of various kinds (this apparently corresponds with the "loud music" called for in aristocratic dances of the English masque). Other scenes show a preponderance of string instruments; examples are the special dance of the swans accompanied by violins *(violini)*, and the dance of twenty-four shepherds, who enter playing violins (probably a simulated performance was intended, since the score calls for an additional forty accompanying instruments at this point).[6]

The Dances

The *Breve Racconto* provides some general information concerning the nature of some of the dances. The final aristocratic dance [17] was supposed to be "graceful and dignified" and was also said to be composed of "floor patterns that were lovely and artful." "Floor patterns" *(figure)* refer to the successive formations assumed by the dancers; for this particular dance, performed by the twenty-four cavaliers, the print offers an illustration (see below), showing various patterns and letters ending with the shape of a heart. Similar patterns were occasionally described in other dance spectacles (masques, ballets, and *intermedii*) of the time.[7] Among the floor patterns the word *intreciata* appears (frame 1), indicating that some form of "interweaving" movement was intended for the dancers. Concerning the other dance diagrams, however, a number of questions arise: Did the shapes have an allegorical significance? How long were the formations held, and what kind of movements took place in between? Do the words *"Secondo"* and *"Terzo Suono"* in frames 3 and 16 mean that the dance was divided into three parts, and that a different number of positions were assumed in each one? If so, *Primo Suono* has two positions; *Secondo Suono* has thirteen positions; and *Terzo Suono* has nine positions.

Curiously, the print informs us that the dances of the swans and of the apes were also comprised of beautiful *figure;* such "imitative" dances (dances that represent the movements of animals) are not usually associated with the aristocratic formations of *figure*. Although no examples of them were included in the sources, these dances appear to be of a different nature than the aristocratic ones, and probably involved pantomime and definite bodily movements. We learn, for instance, that the dance of the swans was to be executed "according to their naturalness" ("secondo il costume della loro naturalezza"), and that the dance of the apes and satyrs contained "gestures after their manner" ("di gesti al lor costume"). The dance of the apes and satyrs was also called "strange" or "extravagant" ("un ballo stravagante"); it involved an element of buffoonery in that the apes were directed to follow and mimic the movements of the satyrs. The dance of Pan and Venus (for which no music has been preserved) must have been a high point in the evening's entertainment. It was a "couple dance and a brilliant display" ("copia e mostra"), and the print tells us (see the Libretto, [15]) it was the one "most worth coming to see" ("più riguardevole").

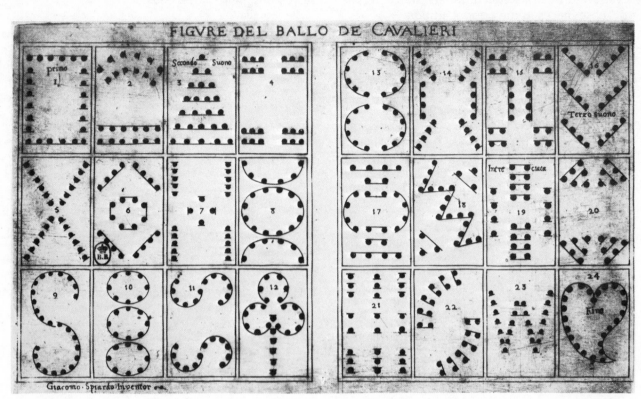

Dance figures for the Cavaliers' dance, No. [17]. The choreographer was Giacomo Spiardo.

The Scheme of this Festa a Ballo

The *festa a ballo* was based on a simple theme, or "device," as it was called in the English masque. Two imaginary realms, the sylvan and oceanic, are represented in the drama, and the beautiful promontory situated near Naples, known as Posilipo, provides the setting (thus the title "The Sylvan and Oceanic Delights of Posilipo"). The sylvan realm, represented by Pan, the satyrs, apes, and shepherds, is grotesque and comical, while the oceanic realm, represented by Venus, Cupid, the swans, and sirens, is serene and graceful. The oceanic creatures are associated with charm and seductiveness. The cavaliers are enchanted by the sirens [5]; then they form a *cortège* around Venus [11]; and their final dance [17] is begun only after Cupid's exhortation, [16]. Meanwhile a confrontation between the sylvan and oceanic realms takes place in [10], when the satyrs pursue the swans; this confrontation prepares the ultimate reconciliation in the couple dance [15] of Pan and Venus.

The *festa a ballo* bears some external resemblance to two *ballets de cour* presented a short time earlier. In *Le Ballet de Monseigneur le Duc de Vendosme* (1610), a miniature palace, noble dancers adorned with jewels, and floor patterns were similarly called for. And *Le Ballet de la Délivrance de Renaud* (1617) includes a "danse burlesque" of the apes, chase scenes, and the use of a set with grottoes; generally, however, this ballet is more complex than the *festa a ballo* as it draws on scenes from Tasso's *Gerusalemme Liberata*.[8]

The Selected Ensemble Pieces from Naples Conservatory MS 4.6.3.

The *festa a ballo* has been supplemented here by the inclusion of several dances (mainly *gagliarde*) for instrumental ensemble selected from a manuscript approximately contemporaneous with the *Breve Racconto*—Naples Conservatory MS 4.6.3.[9] Performances of spectacles like the *festa a ballo* were usually followed by additional dances in which the aristocracy were said to have participated (according to some accounts these "revels" went on far into the night). *Gagliarde* were among the favorite court dances at this time; and the ones included here are simple, note-against-note, utilitarian examples (those by Gesualdo and Trabaci are exceptional in their use of more adventurous harmonies and occasional imitative textures). Selection of dances has been made mainly from the anonymous pieces in the manuscript because such pieces remain unedited elsewhere in modern versions. Additional unedited dances by a composer such as Stella are likely to appear eventually as part of his collected complete works. The contents of MS 4.6.3., originally described with some omissions and inaccuracies in a catalogue of the Conservatorio library,[10] are newly listed here. The chart below gives the original numbering followed by bracketed numbers indicating the order of those pieces in the present edition:[11]

Contents of MS 4.6.3.
R. Conservatorio di San Pietro à Majella, Naples

	Composer	Title	Comments
1 [1]		Sinfonia antica	"Sonata antica" in alto and bass. Divided into "prima, seconda, terza partita," each over the identical bass pattern.
2 [2]		Gagliarda Prima	
3 [3]	[Giovanni da Macque]	Gagliarda Seconda	This piece appears a fourth higher in Ms. Br. Mus. Add. 30491, mod. ed. *Monumenta Musicae Belgicae* IV: 61. Also partially (and at the same pitch) as the middle section of Macque's *Capriccio Sopra un Sogetto, MMB*, IV: 40.
4 [4]		Gagliarda Terza	
5 [5]		Gagliarda Quarta	
6 [6]		Gagliarda Quinta	
7 [7]	[Giovanni Maria Trabaci]	Gagliarda Sesta	"Gagliarda Ottava" in Trabaci's *Ricercate . . .* (Naples, 1603).
8 [8]		Gagliarda Settima	
9 [9]		Gagliarda Ottava	The word "Attacca" appears in the soprano.
10 [10]	[Giovanni Maria Trabaci]	Gagliarda Nona	"Gagliarda Sesta" in Trabaci's *Ricercate . . .* (Naples, 1603).
11 [11]	[Don Carlo Gesualdo]	[Gagliarda]	"Pr[incip]e di Venosa" in Ms. Mod. ed., Glenn Watkins: *Gesualdo di Venosa, Opera Omnia*, vol. X.
12 [12]	Don Giovanni Maria Sabini	Gagliarda Falsa	Sabini was chapelmaster of the Conservatorio Pietà dei Turchini, 1622-6, and organist at the Oratorio dei Filippini in 1630. The meaning of "Falsa" is uncertain.
13	[Scipione] Stella	Prima	
14	[Scipione] Stella	Seconda	
15		folia	After Gagliarda Nona in tenor part. After Stella's Quarta in soprano.
16		La Ciechina	"Cichina" in the bass part. "La Cecchina" was a contemporary reference to Francesca Caccini. The markings "piano" and "forte" appear.
17	[Scipione] Stella	Terza	
18	[Scipione] Stella	Quarta	
19		Pavaniglia	
20 [13]	Hettorre della Marra	Spagnoletta	Bar lines in bass. Nothing is known concerning this composer.
21	Hettorre della Marra	untitled	"a dui soprani"
22 [14]		Gagliarda	
23		Frottola a 3, "Gaude fiore"	
24 [11]	[Don Carlo Gesualdo]	[Basso Continuo]	The lowest part of no. 11 above.
25		Taci bocca	
26		Ave Virgo	
27		[untitled]	
28	[Scipione] Stella	Pange lingua	
29	[Scipione] Stella	O Quam Suavis	
30		Gaude Virgo	
31		Ave Sanctissima Maria	Not in the tenor.
32		Vexilla regis	
33		Gagliarda	
34		[untitled]	
35 [15]	[?] Arpa	Gagliarda	"Spartimento." Perhaps Gioan Leonardo dell'Arpa (mentioned by Cerreto, *Della Pratica Musica*, 1601, p. 158), although the first name looks more like Andrea.
36		Gagliarda a 3	"Spartimento." Text added in soprano: "Magne pater."
37	[?] d'Arpa	Gaude virgo	

Editorial Remarks

Only a single copy has been preserved of each of the two musical sources represented in this volume. The *Breve Racconto* is the source for the *festa a ballo,* and Naples Conservatory MS 4.6.3. is the source of the dances which follow the *festa a ballo.* Thus (except for *gagliarde* by Macque and Trabaci, which are in other sources) concordances were not available. However, both sources appear to be reasonably accurate: the *Breve Racconto* is a carefully prepared print containing relatively few errors; and the manuscript containing the *gagliarde,* despite its appearance of having been hastily assembled, also has only a few equivocal notes. The errors are documented in the Critical Notes.

The editor has suggested certain accidentals (placed in brackets before the note) either to avoid cross relations or to raise a leading tone before a cadence. Occasionally, too, restorative accidentals were deemed necessary for clarification. Parentheses enclose them.

Incipits include the original clef, time signature, subsequent time signature changes, and initial note. The note values of the source for the *festa a ballo* have been maintained, with the exception of the opening piece ("Festa riso"), where they have been halved. The dances of MS 4.6.3. have all been transcribed in a two-to-one reduction. Bar lines generally correspond with those in the sources; editorial bar lines, indicated by dotted lines, appear occasionally to divide double measures.

Two sources for the text of the *festa a ballo* exist: one is the text underlay with the music; the other is the libretto which appears in its own section within the *Breve Racconto.* Certain differences exist between the two; since the libretto text appears to be the more consistent and reliable, it provides the basis for the present edition. Textual underlay is problematic when the supplementary verses of a piece do not appear under the notes themselves but are printed separately. This is especially the case when the number of syllables in a poetic line do not match the notes of the music. In these instances, individual phrases or words of the text have had to be repeated to correspond with the music.

Music is lacking for four of the instrumental pieces in the *festa a ballo* ([6], [8], [10], and [15]). In addition, some question surrounds [4] and [11], which appear in the libretto of *Breve Racconto* together with [17] as "the three dances of the Cavaliers" ("Le tre Arie del Ballo de Cavalieri"); the libretto of the source, however, makes clear the three different appearances of the cavaliers at [4], [11], and [17]. Each one of these dances (called "Aria Prima," "Seconda," "Terza") is therefore made to correspond with the entries of the cavaliers; it is also quite possible, however, that all three dances were intended to be performed as [17] (which would mean that the music for [4] and [11] is lacking).

The word *Aria* for purely instrumental pieces such as these probably derives from certain *Arie per sonare* of the late sixteenth century (e.g., Ingegneri's *Book Two* of 1579 or Facoli's *Book Two* of 1588).

Critical Notes

The following notes record discrepancies between the present edition of the *festa a ballo* and the *Breve Racconto della Festa a Ballo* published in 1620, and between the present edition of the Selected Ensemble Pieces and Naples Conservatory MS 4.6.3. The usual system of pitch designation is used in which middle C is c' and two-line C is c".

Festa a Ballo

No. [3], m. 21, soprano, note 1 is d".
No. [5], m. 34, alto has x before note 2 (g').
No. [13], voice part, m. 105, notes 1-3 are d'.

*The Selected Ensemble Pieces from
Naples Conservatory MS 4.6.3.*

No. [11], mm. 30-1, alto, the editor suggests the double sharp in m. 30 and the f-natural in m. 31 so that a normal chromatic tetrachord is formed from a' to e'.

No. [12], m. 4, soprano, notes 1-2 are c"-sharp; m. 74, soprano, notes 4-5, rhythm is quarter, eighth.

No. [13], m. 9, the notes change when repeated to g' in soprano, d' in alto, and G in bass; m. 21, alto, final note is a whole-note.

No. [14], m. 6, soprano, note 1 is a quarter-note.

No. [15], the name "arpa" could have referred to a composer who played the harp.

Acknowledgments

The editor expresses gratitude to Professor Luigi Tagliavini (Bologna), who brought the existence of the *festa a ballo* to his attention, and to Mrs. Ruth Adams (Northridge, California), who first discovered and communicated to him information concerning MS 4.6.3. The two libraries, the Bibliothèque Nationale in Paris and the Biblioteca del Conservatorio di San Pietro à Majella in Naples, are also to be thanked for kindly making available microfilm versions of the two sources.

Roland Jackson
Claremont Graduate School

January 1978

Notes

1. By Costantino Vitale of Naples. A single copy exists at the Bibliothèque Nationale, Paris. See RISM: *Récueils Imprimés, XVI-XVII Siècles,* I: 472.

2. N. D'Arienzo, *Rivista Musicale Italiana* (1894), I: 389 ff. The print was later mentioned in passing by Ulisse Prota-Giurleo in *Samnium,* I: 85.

3. Contemporary evidence points to Philip's ill health; he died in 1621.

4. Domenico Antonio Parrino, *Teatro Eroico e Politico de'governi de'vicerè del regno di Napoli* (Naples, 1692), II: 92.

5. Pietro Giannone, *The Civil History of the Kingdom of Naples,* trans. James Ogilvie (London, 1731), II: 720 ff.

6. The apparent similarity to the twenty-four violins of the French court is probably coincidental.

7. Some instances are mentioned in John Cutts, "Robert Johnson and the Court Masque," *Music and Letters,* XLI (1960): 112 ff.; and illustrations appear in Paul la Croix, *Ballets et Mascarades de Cour* (Geneva, 1868), p. 265, and in D. P. Walker, *Musique des Intermèdes de la Pellegrina,* p. lvi.

8. See Margaret McGowan, *L'Art du Ballet de Cour en France (1581-1643)* (Paris, 1963).

9. The manuscript is designated 4.6.3. in the R. Conservatorio di San Pietro à Majella, Naples. Although it bears a date of 1629 it contains a repertory extending back to the beginning of the seventeenth century.

10. Guido Gasperini and Franca Gallo, *Città di Napoli, Biblioteca del R. Conservatorio di S. Pietro à Majella* in the series of library catalogues published under the general title *Associazione dei Musicologi Italiani,* X: 2. 550-1 (Parma, 1918).

11. Certain of the indications in the manuscript have proven impossible to decipher and consequently have been omitted. The order of pieces is in accordance with the part books for the bass (the other parts occasionally show a different order).

Text and Translation of the Libretto

The text of the libretto and a line by line translation follow in parallel columns. In the translation, this editor has not aimed at a poetic rendering, but has simply attempted to offer a basic, coherent version that the performer might consult for meaning.

BREVE RACCONTO
DELLA
FESTA A BALLO
Fattasi in Napoli per l'allegrezza della salute
acquistata della Maestà Cattolica di
FILIPPO III. D'AUSTRIA
Rè delle Spagne,
Alla presenza dell'Illustriss. & Eccellentiss.Sig.Duca
d'Ossuna Vicerè del Regno, nella Real Sala di
Palazzo al 1. di Marzo 1620.
IN NAPOLI, Per Costantino Vitale. M.DC.XX.
Et ristampata per Tarquinio Longo.

A BRIEF REPORT
OF THE
DANCE FESTIVAL
that took place in Naples in celebration of the health
regained by His Catholic Majesty,
PHILIP III OF AUSTRIA,
King of the Spains.
In the presence of the most illustrious and excellent Duke
of Ossuna, the Viceroy of the Kingdom, in the royal hall of
the palace on March 1, 1620.
Published IN NAPLES by Costantino Vitale, 1620,
and reprinted by Tarquinio Longo.

[PARTICIPANTS]

La presente Festa in allegrezza della sa-/lute acquistata della Maestà Cattolica,/fu fatta da D. Alvaro di Mendozza Ca-/stellano del Castel novo, in compagnia/di ventitre Cavalieri, da i quali fu con-/venuto, che frà tutti loro se n'eliggessero/dodeci a sorte per disporre l'ordine dell'uscite al ballo;/e che ciascheduno d'essi eletti successivamente nella sua/elettione chiamasse il suo compagno, e furono i seguenti./

The present festivity, in celebration of the health regained by His Catholic Majesty, was performed by Don Alvaro di Mendozza, the Governor of the Castel Nuovo, in the company of twenty-three Cavaliers, among whom it has been agreed upon that they should elect from among themselves by lot the twelve to set the order of departure to the dance, and that each of those elected should in succession upon his election call out his companion; and they were the following.

Il Castellano D. Alvaro di Mendozza, e D. Antonio di/Mendozza Conte di Gambatesa suo Zio./Il Duca di Santolia, & il Conte della Rocchetta./D. Francesco Caracciolo d'Ettorre, e D. Ottavio Cantelmo./Cesare Galluccio, & il Marchese di Cusano./Il Principe di Conca, e Lelio Filomarino./Paolo Spinello, e Francesco Pignatello./ Il Principe di Sanzi, e D. Gio. Girone/D. Carlo Sanseverino, e D. Michel Cavaniglia./ D. Gaspar Toraldo, & il Marchese d'Anzi./Il Cav. Frà Ferrante Rocco, e D. Carlo Carafa di Bitetto./Francesco Brancia, e Gio. Battista Caracciolo d'Alfonsetto./Il Duca di Termini, e Gio. Paolo del Dolce./

The Governor Don Alvaro di Mendozza, and Don Antonio di Mendozza the Count of Gambatesa, his uncle. The Duke of Santolia, and the Count of Rocchetta. Don Francesco Caracciolo d'Ettorre, and Don Ottavio Cantelmo. Cesare Galluccio, and the Marquis of Cusano. The Prince of Conca, and Lelio Filomarino. Paolo Spinello, and Francesco Pignatello. The Prince of Sanzi, and Don Giovanni Girone. Don Carlo Sanseverino, and Don Michel Cavaniglia. Don Gaspar Toraldo, and the Marquis of Anzi. The Cavalier Brother Ferrante Rocco, and Don Carlo Carafa of Bitetto. Francesco Brancia, and Giovanni Battista Caracciolo d'Alfonsetto. The Duke of Termini, and Giovanni Paolo del Dolce.

[STAGE SETTING]

L'inventione dell'apparato, fu il delizioso monte di/POSILIPO, formandosi particolarmente tutto di ri-/lievo il Palazzo detto della Goletta luogo dell' istesso/Castellano in Posilipo, & i suoi giardini, scogli, e grot-/te fuori, e dentro de'quali si rappresentò la vaghezza/della sua marina mobile con pesci guizzanti, il tutto/con l'istessa vaghezza, che nel detto POSILIPO si/gode con mirabile artifitio tutto al naturale, e con/diversità di canti d'ucelli, e dolci suoni d'istromenti,/e di canti.

The stage setting is the delightful mountain of POSILIPO, which sets off the palace, called the Gorge, the place of residence of the said Governor in Posilipo, and its gardens, ledges, and grottoes, behind and in front of which is represented the beauty of the sea-coast, alive with darting fish, everything with the same beauty that can be enjoyed in Posilipo itself, with remarkable artifice just as in nature, and with a diversity of bird-songs and the sweet sounds of instruments and of singing.

Gli Abiti de'Cavalieri del ballo furono tutti di concer-/to di lama d'argento foderati, & riccamati di cremesi-/no, e d'argento; tempestati di pietre acquemarine, che/dimostravano esser tutte cariche di gioielli, con col-/letti di felpa d'oro in forma di dante, & cappelli di Ca-/storo con grossi cordoni d'oro, gioe, & molte penne, e/con pistole á lato, e tutta la forma dell'habito fù di/campagna.

The garments of the Cavaliers participating in the dance were all harmonious, with swords lined with silver and embroidered in crimson and silver, adorned with aquamarine stones, that gave the impression that they were loaded with jewels, with collars of golden plush in the form of buckskin, and beaver hats with great golden cords, jewels, and many feathers, and with pistols in holsters, and everything about the garments appearing rustic.

Et anco tutti personaggi operanti nell'inventione com/parvero con la proprietà de gli habiti loro ricchi, e va-/gamente vestiti./

And also everyone participating on stage appeared appropriately attired in rich and attractive garments.

[The Text]

Delizie di Posilipo Boscarecce,/e Maritime.

The Sylvan and Oceanic Delights of Posilipo.

Compaiono tre Ninfe con un Pastore sopra lo scoglio/della Goletta, delizioso palazzo in Posilipo, e/cantano la seguente Canzonetta.

Three Nymphs and a Shepherd appear above the ledge of the Gorge, the delightful palace in Posilipo, and sing the following little song.

[1.]

Festa, riso, gioco, e gioia
Son quest'onde, e questo monte;
Tutti han quì le Gratie pronte,
Nè v'è duol, mestitia, ò noia.
Quì dal monte al mar sonoro
Fan gli augelli eterno canto,
A cui van danzando intanto
L'ombre, e l'aure, e'l mar fra loro.
Le delizie, e in un gli Amori
Seggi han quì giocondi, e cari;
Qui Natura, e'l Cielo al pari
Versar tutti i lor tesori.

[1.]

Festive, laughing, playing, and joyful
are these waves and this mountain.
Everyone here has the Graces at hand;
here is no sorrow, grief, or misfortune.
Here resounding from mountain to sea
the birds make lasting song,
to which at the same time dance
the shadows, breezes, and sea among themselves.
[All] delights and loves together
have here their dear and joyful seats;
here nature and heaven equally
have poured out all their treasures.

[2.] Sebeto ragiona

[2.] Sebeto discourses

[This lengthy dedicatory poem to the Viceroy, Don Pedro Giron the Duke of Ossuna, is delivered in spoken form by an actor costumed as Sebeto, a water sprite. The English version offers a prose paraphrase. Many of the lines are difficult to render in an exact translation; and indeed, the poem in general can perhaps be fully grasped only within the context of the political or social climate of the *seicento* Neapolitan court.]

Se vicino allo splendore di si leggiadre Dame (Gene-/rosissimo Principe) dalle Stelle de'begli occhi loro/incoronato questo bel monte si vagamente risplende, chi/non dirà ch'egli sia il famosissimo Atlante? mentre hog-/gi anco voi reggete suo degno, & invitto Alcide, il peso di/sì bel CIELO. E chi più oltre investigando contempla,/qual anco in esso si formi dal vostro real Destriero, fatto/via più vago, e celebre Pegaso, di vostre gratie abbondan-/tissimo fonte; non crederà, ch'egli sia il si lodato Parnaso,/le cui Muse à celebrar vostre lodi son dolci cantatrici Si-/rene, il cui fiorito sentiero da i raggi del vostro aspetto,/come un più lucido Febo con vaghi smalti s'indora, e pu-/re ancor ch'egli sembri il famosissimo Atlante, o'l si lo-/dato Parnaso, altro egli non è, che'l delizioso PAUSI-/LIPPO, in cui sempre sono amichevolmente conformi con/la vaghezza de' suoi teneri smeraldi, la serenitá di quest'a-/ria, la tranquillità di quest'onde, ne' cui chiari, e mobili cri-/stalli ogn'hora vagh-

In paragraph one (lines 1-20) Sebeto offers homage by first comparing the mountain (perhaps the mountain represented on stage or perhaps the mountain of Naples) with Atlantis. Then Giron is likened to Alcide and to Phoebus; while his steed, from which he bestows benefits to the populace, is likened to the celebrated Pegasus. Thereupon Sebeto compares the local setting with Parnassus, whose Muses, now taking the form of sweetly singing Sirens, also lavish praises upon Giron. Sebeto then reveals that Atlantis, or Parnassus, is indeed nothing other than the delightful Posilipo (i.e., the attractive terrain and mountainside close to Naples), a place whose serene air and crystal waves can nowhere be matched.

eggiandosi il monte, sembra che si con-/sigli tra fioriti ricami qual de' suoi propri pregi altrui pom-/poso in bella mostra s'adorni, & il più vago delle sue parti/disponga.

Quindi in si bel quadro d'acque forma dal suo/vivo ritrato nel mare un prato, e in un bel mar di verd'om-/bre, onde di fiori. La onde in perpetua primauera albergo/è di diletti, vago specchio del Cielo, eterno giardino del-/la natura, paradiso di gioia, felice stanza delle Grazie,/lieta sede d'Amore, bel seggio del vostro Impero, e gloriosissima/base del tempio della nostra Fama.

Quì dun-/que per questo mar Tirheno, giungendo hor'io picciol/SEBETO d'acque, ma di fè grande, sospendo il corso,/miro, anzi ammiro, com'hoggi il tutto quì belle Donne/per voi fuor dell'usato à marauiglia s'accresca in qualità/più dilettosa, e gioconda, virtú sola del vostro viso, for-/za sola de'bei vostr'occhi. E mentre apprestano a voi Fa-/moso, & Eroico Principe questi miei cari figli habitatori/ del monte per effetto del loro affetto, in tributo del loro/amore, trà dolci suoni, e canti artificiose, e leggiadre/danze;

godo d'udir quì d'intorno il vostro nome, come/celebrato s'honori, & honorato s'ammiri. Ma chi sarà/quel, che non goda, poiche tutti allegri per l'acquista-/ta, salute del nostro Rè festeggiamo rimirando già quel/gran CIELO, che d'atre nubi sgombratosi sereno hor/mostra il bel sembiante, e lucide le sue Stelle, a'cui/reali, e benigni influssi ad esser lietamente soggeti for-/tunati nascono i mondi, al qual serenissimo CIEL. O so-/lo quell'Aquila giunge, che sovrastando ad ogn'alto,/e sublime volo, non già ministra, ma toglie di mano al-/l'Hispano Giove i folgori del suo sdegno, e sotto l'om-/bra delle sue grand'ali sicuro, e certo ricovro altrui sem-/pre presta generosamente pietosa, dal qual luminoso/CIELO há il suo splendore il vostro lume, e frà i gran/segni della sua luce há il vostro Sole il suo gran GIRO.

Onde il nostro monte, se di ricever lungamente sia degno/dal vostro splendidissimo Sole i raggi d'immortal vita,/vedrassi com'egli sempre al vostro glorioso crine trion-/fali allori produca, & alla vostra invitta destra palme vit-/toriose consacri./Tal sempre il nostro Ciel voi esser vide/Febo al suo lume, al suo sostegno Alcide.

Fortuna, Tempo, Fama, & Invidia uscendo in/barca cantano.

[3.]
Nel gran GIRON s'uniro
Com'in stellato GIRO,
Fama, Tempo, Fortuna, e Invidia insieme,
Che gli hà soggetti, e il lor poter non teme.
A cui la Fama hor dice,
Piu mondi haver ne lice,
Ch'al tuo vanto un sol mondo esser gia miro
Un picciol centro entr'al tuo nobil GIRO.
Cui dice il Tempo ancora,
Pera pur altri, e mora,
Ch'al tuo nome immortal la vita aggiro
Con farmi eterno entr'al tuo nobil GIRO.
A cui Fortuna amante
Dice in caro sembiante,
A liete imprese, e a gran vittorie io giro
La mia gran rota entr'al tuo nobil GIRO.
A cui l'Invidia al fine
Bench'à forza s'inchine,

In paragraph two (lines 21-7) this lovely region is further described. The terrain impresses its image upon the surrounding waters in such a way that the sea takes on the appearance of a veritable meadow of flowers. Such a garden, formed now upon the waves, has become the seat of the empire over which Giron rules.

In paragraph three (lines 28-37) Sebeto marvels at how the ladies present in the audience receive their great virtue from Giron's face and their strength from his eyes. The ladies who participate in the spectacle, on the other hand, are enabled to return both esteem and affection to Giron through their most artful singing and graceful dancing.

In paragraph four (lines 38-51) Sebeto expresses his pleasure that the King of the Spains (King Philip III) has recently regained his health. And then, after referring to the serenity of Neapolitan skies, to its stars, and its planets, he compares Giron to a lofty eagle, who, soaring in flight above the city, receives from the Hispanic Jove (i.e., Philip III) lightning bolts of wrath, but at the same time affords both generosity and compassion from beneath his protective wings. Giron is indeed a sun whose course ("*giro*") traverses the Neapolitan skies.

In paragraph five (lines 52-7) the mountain of Posilipo is shown to have received its very sustenance from such a sun. In return, the people of Naples have bestowed the laurels and the palms of victory on the viceroy Giron. The sky above Naples belongs to him; he is a Phoebus who creates its light, an Alcide who gives it its sustenance.

Fortune, Time, Fame, and Envy sing, going out in a barque:

[3.]
In great GIRON is united
as in a starry COURSE
Fame, Time, and Fortune, together with Envy.
These he has as his subjects, and of their power he has no
   fear.
To him Fame now says:
Further worlds you may have;
I already behold a single world to be to your glory.
Like a small center, it enters upon your noble COURSE.
To him Time also says:
Perish, then, and die [you] others.
Since I will connect life to your immortal name,
by making myself eternal, I enter upon your noble
   COURSE.
To him beloved Fortune
Says in dearest semblance:
I turn upon happy actions and great victories;
My great wheel enters upon your noble COURSE.

Dice anco astretta i tuoi gran merti ammiro
Con dolce incanto entr'al tuo nobil GIRO.
Nel gran GIRON s'uniro
Com'in stellato GIRO
Fama, Tempo, Fortuna, e Invidia insieme
Che gli hà soggetti, e il lor poter non teme.

To him at last Envy,
Although inclined to violence,
Also says restrainedly: I will admire your great merits;
As though enchanted I will enter upon your noble
    COURSE.
In great GIRON is united,
As in starry COURSE,
Fame, Time, and Fortune, together with Envy.
These he has as his subjects, and of their power he has no
    fear.

Scendono i ventiquattro Cavalieri dal monte, accom-/pagnati da gran quantità d'istromenti, & en-/trano nella Goletta senza esser poi/veduti fuori

The twenty-four Cavaliers descend from the mountain to the accompaniment of a large number of instruments; they enter into the Gorge so as not to be seen from outside.

[4. Aria Prima]

[4. First Aria]

Compariscono tre Sirene, una esce dal destro lato della/Goletta fuori d'una grotta, l'altra dal sinistro d'un al-/tra grotta, e la terza sorge dal mare nel mezo, cantan-/do insieme con dolce suono d'istromenti,

Three Sirens appear; one enters from the right side of the Gorge out of a grotto, another from the left out of another grotto, and the third, rising from the sea, in the middle; they sing together accompanied by the sweet sound of instruments:

[5. Arie di tre Sirene]

A Voi famoso Eroe divote, e pronte
In dì si caro, e lieto
Noi Sirene, e Sebeto
Dar vogliam tributarii al vostro vanto
Puro cor, vera fede, e dolce canto;

[5. Arias of the three Sirens]

Devoted to you, famous Hero, and ready
On this day, so dear and joyful,
We Sirens, and Sebeto,
Wish to offer tributes to your fame,
[to] your pure heart, your true faith, and [we also sing] sweet
    song.

A voi che sol rendete
Lieto Sebeto, e le Sirene liete
A voi di questo grato ameno monte

To you who alone make
Sebeto and the Sirens happy;
To you, the deity of this joyful and pleasant mountain,

Di questo gentil Fiume
Caro terreno nume;
Bel Sol del nostro Ciel vago, e sereno,
E gran Nettuno a noi del mar Tirrheno,
E benche ài nostri incanti il Ciel prescrisse
D'esser voi cauto Ulisse,

Of this gentle stream,
And of this dear terrain;
[You are] the beautiful sun in our lovely and serene sky,
And to us the great Neptune of the Tirrhenian sea.
And although heaven prescribes,
That you, Ulysses, should be wary of our enchantments,

Oggi l'incanto sia pari fra noi

The enchantment may actually go both ways today,

Voi d'esser grato à Noi, noi grati à Voi.
A voi, che per valore
Sempre Proteo d'honore
In vaghe forme il mondo esser vi vide
Nume, Febo, Nettuno, Ulisse, Alcide.

So that you may be gracious toward us, just as we are to-
    ward you.
Because of your valor,
Forever most-honored Proteus,
The world assumes its beautiful forms,
Deity, Phoebus, Neptune, Ulysses, Alcide.

Compariscono i ventiquattro Cavalieri à vista di tutti/disposti in ordinanza in una loggia della Goletta ascol-/tando le cantatrici Sirene.

The twenty-four Cavaliers reappear so as to be seen by everyone; they group themselves on a terrace of the Gorge, and listen to the singing Sirens.

Finiscono il canto le Sirene, e rientrano per la medema/via, intanto i Caualieri tirati dal canto scendono à/seguirle, & entrati nelle grotte non si veggono.

When they have finished their song, the Sirens exit as they came in; at the same time the Cavaliers, drawn by their song, descend in order to follow them; after they have entered the grottoes, they cannot be seen.

Poi suonano le ciaramelle dandosi un poco d'intervallo.

Next the shawms play, providing a short interlude.

Scende dal monte il Dio Pane con tre Silvani, accompa-/gnati da sei Selvaggi, e sei Scimie à suono di sordelli-/ne, e restano dietro la Goletta.

The god Pan descends from the mountain with three sylvan creatures, accompanied by six Satyrs, and six Apes, to the sound of bagpipes and they remain behind the Gorge.

[6.]

[6. Entrance of Pan—no music in source]

In questo escono da due altre grotte ventiquattro Pastori/ con istromenti di violini, e si dispongono in ordine/ne' loro palchi.

Then twenty-four Shepherds enter from two other grottoes with in-struments of the violin family, and arrange themselves on their scaffolds.

[7.] Il suono della scesa de' Pastori dal monte su'l ponte sonato da quaranta vary istromenti detta la Mendozza

[7.] Musical number for the descent of the Shepherds from the mountain onto the bridge, played by forty instruments of various kinds and called la Mendozza

[8.]

[8. Exit of Pan—no music in source]

Appresso suonando esce Pane coi sopradetti Silvani,/Sel-vaggi, e Scimie ponendosi in prospettiva nella me-/desima loggia della Goletta, in cui si videro prima i Cavalieri.

A little later Pan enters with the above-mentioned sylvan creatures, Satyrs, and Apes, who place themselves in view on the same terrace of the Gorge in which the Cavaliers were first seen.

Sonando gl'istromenti di dentro, esce Venere dal mare/in una ricca Conca con Amore in seno tirata da Cigni,/e seco escono da i lati otto Cigni, quattro per parte,/e canta;

Accompanied by instruments from behind, Venus issues from the sea in a sumptuous shell, with Cupid at her bosom; they are drawn by Swans; and with them eight [other] Swans enter, four from each side; and [Venus] sings:

[9. Aria de Venere]

Donne mie care,
Che n'acquistate
Ciò, che mirate,
Ciò, che si vede,
Ch'Amor possede.
Qual de' vostr'occhi
Feri, ò benigni
Spiegano i Cigni
Con dolce canto
Le glorie, e'l vanto;
Tal hoggi, inanzi
De'i lor bei giri
Con vaghi giri
Voi vagheggiando,
Vadan danzando.
A voi gl'invio,
Ch'a dilettarvi,
Com'à lodarvi
Conformi sono
Al canto, e al suono.

[9. Aria of Venus]

My dear ladies,
Who [are able to] obtain
Those things which you admire,
Those things which are seen,
Which Cupid possesses.
Those things [that are] in your eyes,
Proud or gracious,
The Swans [can] explain
Through [their] sweet song,
Your glories and your pride;
Thus today, before
their beautiful pirouettes,
With lovely turns,
Gazing upon you with delight,
They move in dance.
To you I send them
So as to delight you,
As well as to praise you,
They are in conformity
In song, and [musical] playing.

Finito di cantar Venere, per la medesima via, ch'uscirono/ se n'entrano i Cigni./Entrati i Cigni, scendono dalla Goletta i Seluaggi, e le/Scimie à seguirgli, restando sù la loggia à suonare il/Dio Pane con i Silvani.

When Venus has finished her song, the Swans enter by the same way as they had [earlier] departed. After the Swans have entered, the Sa-tyrs and the Apes descend from the Gorge and pursue them, while the god Pan and the sylvan creatures remain on the ledge in order to play their instruments.

[10.]

[10. Music of Pan and Sylvan Creatures—no music in source]

Escono poi a suon di trombe dalle due grotte di fronte/i ventiquattro Cavalieri su'l ponte à prendere in me-/zo [sic] Venere.

Then the twenty-four Cavaliers enter from the two front grottoes ac-companied by the sounding of trumpets; they proceed onto the bridge to form a cortège around Venus.

[11. Aria Seconda]

[11. Second Aria]

Usciti i Cavalieri, escono dalle due grotte di basso i Ci-/gni à far un balletto di molte varie, e belle figure com-/poste secondo il costume della loro naturalezza; e dan-/zanno à vista de'Cavalieri.

After the Cavaliers have made their exit, the Swans enter from the two lowest grottoes to execute a dance of many varied and beautiful patterns in accordance with their naturalness; and they dance in view of the Cavaliers.

[12.] Suono del Ballo de Cigni, sonato da violini

[12.] The dance of the Swans, played by violins

Finito il ballo de'Cigni cantano il Dio Pane, & i suoi/Silvani dalla loggia.

After the dance of the Swans, the god Pan and his sylvan creatures sing [about Posilipo] from the ledge:

[13.]

Lenguas son deste monte piedras, y plantas
Que alabando hermosuras milagros cantan.

Lenguas son destas playas ondas, y flores
Que si occultan desleos cantan amores.

Mas siente el monte,
Mas sienta, y pene.

Que cuydados de amores montes los sienten,
Que si alaba hermosuras, es bien que sienta,
Que aunque son ynfinitas, son pocas lenguas.

Oy Pauxilipo, que adora
Tanta hermosura procura
Publicar, que la hermosura
Aun los montes enamora.

Pero quanto pinta, y dora
El sol en su falda verde,
Veldad pierde;
Si compitiendo os retrata,

Si dilata
Por estas cumbras sus flores,
Lenguas, que cantan amores,

Rusticas son si no cuentan,
Que aunque son ynfinitas,
son pocas lenguas.

El mar, que en candida espuma
Perlas, coral, plata ofrece
Humilde, y pobre parece,
Aunque mas riquezas suma

Puzol, Baya, Enaria, y Cuma
Esmeraldas, y Zafiros
En olas como en suspiros
Os presentan;

Mas se afrentan,
Que al culto de tal Deydad
Todo pierde su veldad;

Pues si os alaban confiesan,
Que aunque son ynfinitas,
son pocas lenguas,

Lenguas son deste monte....

Havendo cantato Pane, & i Silvani, escono dall'istesse/ grotte di basso i sei Selvaggi à far un'altro balletto di/gesti al lor costume, e seguendogli sei Scimie imitan-/do ancor'esse le mutanze del ballo de'Selvaggi, fanno/unitamente i Selvaggi, & le Scimie un ballo strava-/gante.

[14.] Suono del Ballo de' Selvaggi, e delle Simie, sonato da istromenti di fiato

Pertanto furono duo Numi i Capi, e dispensieri di quan-/to fè la Festa più riguardevole, Pane cioè, e Venere:/quegli delle boschereccie, questa delle maritime va-/ghezze facendo copia, e mostra.

[1] A volcanic rock indigenous to the region of Naples.
[2] *Baya* may also refer to a berry (Lat. *bacca*).
[3] The meaning of *enaria* is unknown to this editor.
[4] The *cuma* is a plant indigenous to Brazil.

[13.]

The rocks and plants of this mountain are [like] tongues, which, in praising [your] beauties, sing of miracles.

The waves and flowers of these shores are [like] tongues that sing of love, although they conceal indiscretions.

The more the mountain feels [these things] the more it suffers and grieves,

Because the mountains feel the cares of love. For if [the mountain] praises beauties, it is well that it feels, for although they [the beauties] are infinite, they are [still too] few tongues.

O Posilipo, that adores so much beauty, try to make it known that your beauty even enamors the mountains.

But howevermuch the sun paints and gilds in its verdant foothills, it loses [its] beauty if it vies to portray you,

[if] it expends on these summits its flowers, tongues that sing of love.

They are unmannerly if they do not admit, that although they are infinite, they are [still too] few tongues.

The sea, which in its white foam offers pearls, coral, and silver, appears to be lowly and poor, yet it adds up to great riches:

Pozzolana,[1] star of Bethlehem,[2] *enaria*,[3] *cuma*,[4] emeralds and sapphires, in waves as in sighs are offered to you.

But they are affronted, that in the worship of such a Deity, everything loses its beauty.

Since in praising you they confess that although they are infinite, they are [still too] few tongues.

The rocks and plants of this mountain are like tongues....

After Pan and the sylvan creatures have finished their singing, the six Satyrs enter from the same low grottoes to execute another dance of gestures according to their manner; and they are followed by six Apes, imitating the movements of the dance of the Satyrs; the Satyrs and Apes together execute a "fantastic" dance.

[14.] Dance of the Satyrs and Apes, played by wind instruments

However, two gods were the principal ones, and the stewards of that which makes the festival most worth seeing: Pan, that is, and Venus, the former of the sylvan, the latter of the oceanic realm, beautifully danced a duet and [presented] a spectacle.

Finito questo, Amore, che stà nella Conca con Venere/presenta alle Dame il ballo de i ventiquattro Cavalie-/ri, che fan corona cantando la seguente canzonetta.

[16. Cupido solo dice]

Da quest'acque,
Da cui nacque
Mia gran madre, e chiara Dea,
Citerea;
Ch'arde il mondo in questo loco

Del mio foco;
A voi sorgo,
E vi porgo
Queste schiere, e questi amanti
Festeggianti,
Vaghe Donne; e sol sostegno
Del mio regno.
In lor scocchi
Da'vostr'occhi
Sol quel stral, la cui ferita
Gli da vita,
E sanar può la mortale
Del mio strale.
Dunque liete
Ricevete
Questi amanti, a la cui fede
Fia mercede
L'acquistar sol nel servirvi
Di gradirvi.

[17. Aria Terza]

Dopo che hà cantato Amore, scendono i ventiquattro/Cavalieri a danzare in sala vagamente vestiti, e fanno/un ballo leggiadramente grave di molte vaghe, & ar-/tificiose figure, e si dà fine.

[15. Dance of Pan and Venus—no music in source]

After this, Cupid, who is standing in the shell with Venus, presents the dance of the twenty-four Cavaliers to the Ladies, who "crown" [the evening]; and he sings the following little song:

[16. Cupid alone says]

From these waters
From which I had my birth,
My great mother, and dear goddess,
Cythera;
[I had my birth] that all here present might be enflamed

By my fire.
To you I arise,
And offer you
These troupes and these loving gentlemen,
Celebrating
The lovely Ladies, the sole support
Of my reign.
In the beams
Of your eyes,
Only that ray that wounds
Gives life,
And mortal man can be healed
By my rays.
Therefore, happily
Receive
These gentleman lovers, for whose faith
You should give thanks,
The acquiring [of which comes] only from serving,
Of pleasing you.

[17. Third Aria]

After Cupid has sung, the twenty-four Cavaliers, elegantly dressed, descend to dance in the hall, and they execute a gracefully solemn dance, of many lovely and artful formations; and [the spectacle] there ends.

[STAGE DESIGNER, COMPOSERS, AND CHOREOGRAPHER]

Il disegno, & architettura del monte, della marina, delle/grotte, e del palazzo della Goletta, e d'altre apparenze/rappresentate, fu fatto per Bartolomeo Cartaro Regio/Ingegnero delli Castelli del Regno di Napoli.

La musica del canto delle Ninfe, e del Pastore sopra le/parole, Festa, riso, gioco, &c. Fù fatta da Pietro Anto-/nio Giramo./La musica del canto della Fama, Fortuna, Tempo, & In-/vidia, sopra le parole. Nel gran Giron s'uniro, &c./Fù fatta da Francesco Lambardi./La musica del canto delle Sirene sopra le parole./A voi Famoso Eroe, &c. Fù fatta da Gio. Maria Trabace./La musica del canto del Dio Pane; e Silvani sopra le pa-/role. Lenguas son deste monte, &c. Fù fatta da Fran-/cesco Lambardi. La musica del canto di Venere sopra le parole, Donne/mie care, &c. Fù fatta da Gio. Maria Trabace./La musica del canto d'Amore sopra le parole, Da que-/st'acque, &c. Fù fatta da Francesco Lambardi.

The design and stage set of the mountain, the sea, the grottoes, and the building of the Gorge, and other represented appearances were made by Bartolomeo Cartaro, royal engineer of the Castles of the Kingdom of Naples.

The music of the song of the Nymphs and Shepherds, on the words "Festa, riso, gioco," etc., was composed by Pietro Antonio Giramo. The music of the song of Fame, Fortune, Time, and Envy, on the words "Nel gran Giron s'uniro," etc., was composed by Francesco Lambardi. The music of the song of the Sirens, on the words "A voi Famoso Eroe," etc., was composed by Giovanni Maria Trabaci. The music of the song of the god Pan and the sylvan deities, on the words "Lenguas son deste monte," etc., was composed by Francesco Lambardi. The music of the song of Venus, on the words "Donne mie care," etc., was composed by Giovanni Maria Trabaci. The music of the song of Cupid, on the words "Da quest'acque," etc., was composed by Francesco Lambardi.

Il suono del ballo de'Cigni./Il suono del ballo de'Selvaggi, e delle Scimie. Furono/composti da Giacomo Spiardo.

The music of the dance of the Swans, and of the dance of the Satyrs and Apes, was composed by Giacomo Spiardo.

Il suono della scesa de'violini su'l Ponte./Le tre arie del ballo de'Cavalieri si fecero da Andrea/Ansalone.

The music of the descent of the violins on the bridge and the three dance arias of the Cavaliers was composed by Andrea Ansalone.

Delle figure del ballo de'Cigni, de'gesti, e figure del bal-/lo de'Selvaggi, Scimie, e delle loro stravaganze, e/delle figure, e vaghi andamenti del ballo de'Cavalieri/ne fù l'inventore il detto Giacomo Spiardo.

The inventor of the patterns of the dance of the Swans, of the gestures and patterns of the dance of the Satyrs and Apes, and of their "extravagant" gestures, and of the patterns and lovely movements of the dance of the Cavaliers, was the said Giacomo Spiardo.

Avertendosi che per breuità si tralasciano le figure del/ballo de'Cigni, de'Selvaggi, e delle Scimie.

Note that for the sake of brevity the patterns of the dance of the Swans, and of the Satyrs and Apes have been omitted.

[CONCLUDING DEDICATORY POEM TO THE LADIES]

De'bei vostr'occhi à tanti almi splendori
Fassi il Ciel di Zafiro ò Donne belle;

O beautiful Ladies, from your lovely eyes, those life-giving splendors, I could have created a sky [filled] with sapphires.

E questo mar lucido Ciel di stelle.

And [I could have created] this lucid sea, [which is like] a heaven of stars.

Fa l'herbe di smeraldo, e d'oro i fiori.

It [the ocean] makes foliage out of emeralds, flowers of gold.

Questo bel monte, e questa riva amena
Di minuti diamanti empie l'arena.

The sand fills this lovely mountain and this pleasing shore with tiny diamonds.

Qui l'ombre, e l'aure a dilettarvi ogn'hora

Here are shade and breezes to delight you at all times.

Fredde per gelosia rivali amanti

It [the shade] cools lovers, [who are] rivals through jealousy.

Carche d'odor ballan d'augelli ai canti;

They [the breezes], charged with fragrances, dance to the singing of birds.

D'Agate rivestiti anco inamora
Amor gli scogli a darvi pretiosi
Sù diaspri, e rubin seggi pomposi:

Love again inspires the sea cliffs, [which are] invested with agate stones, that they might give you precious things, stately thrones [built] upon jaspers and rubies.

Disfatto in perle in cosi ricche sponde
Vi mostra amando il mar, qual si consume
D'amaro pianto in cristalline spume.

The sea, undone [in breaking waves] on the pearls upon such wealthy shores, reveals itself lovingly to you, [the sea] that consumes itself with a bitter lament in the crystalline foam.

Quindi amante co'l mar l'acque confonde
Piangendo il monte, e sembrano à vederle
Liquidi argenti uniti a molli perle.

Thence the lover confounds lamentingly the mountain with the waters of the sea, and they [the mountain and the waters] seem to see the silvery liquids united with the delicate pearls.

Miransi i pesci in cosi gran tesoro
Con le smaltate squame, e di coralli
Il capo ornar fra i mobili cristalli.

The fish, with their enameled scales, regard themselves in such a great treasure [i.e., in these beautiful surroundings], to adorn the coral cape among the moving crystals.

Seguon del vostro crin le reti d'oro
Guizzando amanti, e dove Vener nacque,
Senza spegner l'ardore ardon ne l'acque,

They [the fish] pursue the golden nets of your tresses, [like] darting lovers, and without allaying their ardor in the waters, [in the very waters] in which Venus was born.

Mentre abellito il tutto ama, e s'accende
Al sol de'bei vostr'occhi, il Sol vien meno,
Cedendo lor de la sua luce il freno.

While everything is beautified, loves, and is kindled by the sunlight of your beautiful eyes, [and compared with this sunlight] the sun [itself] shines less brightly, surrendering to them [your eyes], a restraining of its light.

E cede il mio bel Sol, che frà voi splende

And my lovely Sun, which shines among you [now also] subsides.

PARTENOPE la bella a i rai maggiori
De'bei vostr'occhi i suoi almi splendori.

PARTHENOPE [i.e., Naples], the beautiful [also accedes] to the greater rays of your beautiful eyes, [offering] its own life-giving splendors.

IL FINE

THE END

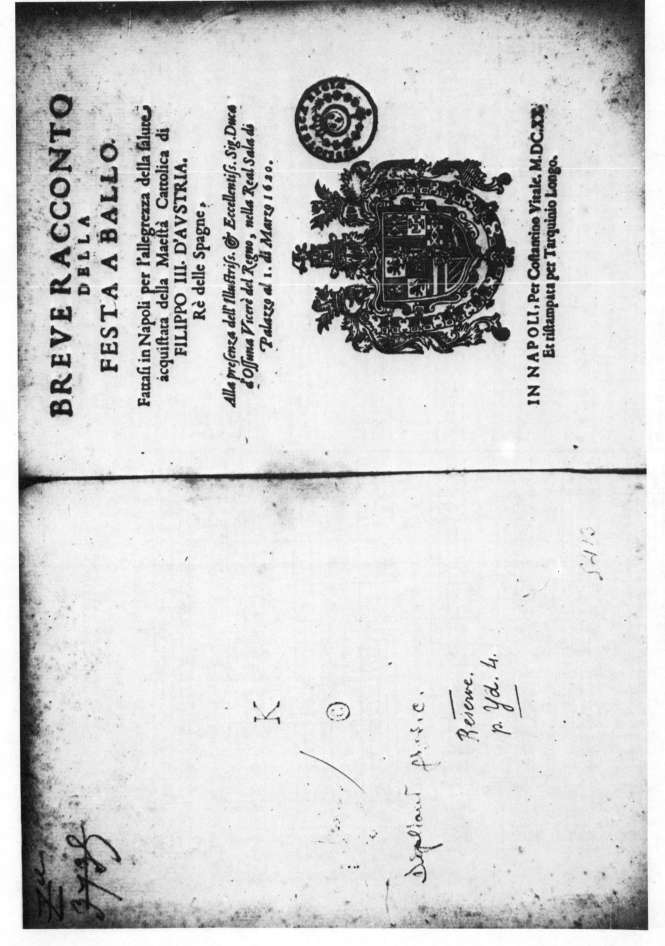

BREVE RACCONTO
DELLA
FESTA A BALLO.

Fattasi in Napoli per l'allegrezza della salute
acquistata della Maestà Cattolica di
FILIPPO III. D'AVSTRIA.
Rè delle Spagne,

*Alla presenza dell'Illustriss. & Eccellentiss. Sig. Duca
d'Ossuna Vicerè del Regno, nella Real Sala di
Palazzo al 1. di Marzo 1620.*

IN NAPOLI, Per Costantino Vitale. M.DC.XX.
Et ristampata per Tarquinio Longo.

Plate I. Title page of the *Breve Racconto della Festa a Ballo.*
The sole copy of this print is in the possession of the Bibliothèque Nationale, Paris.

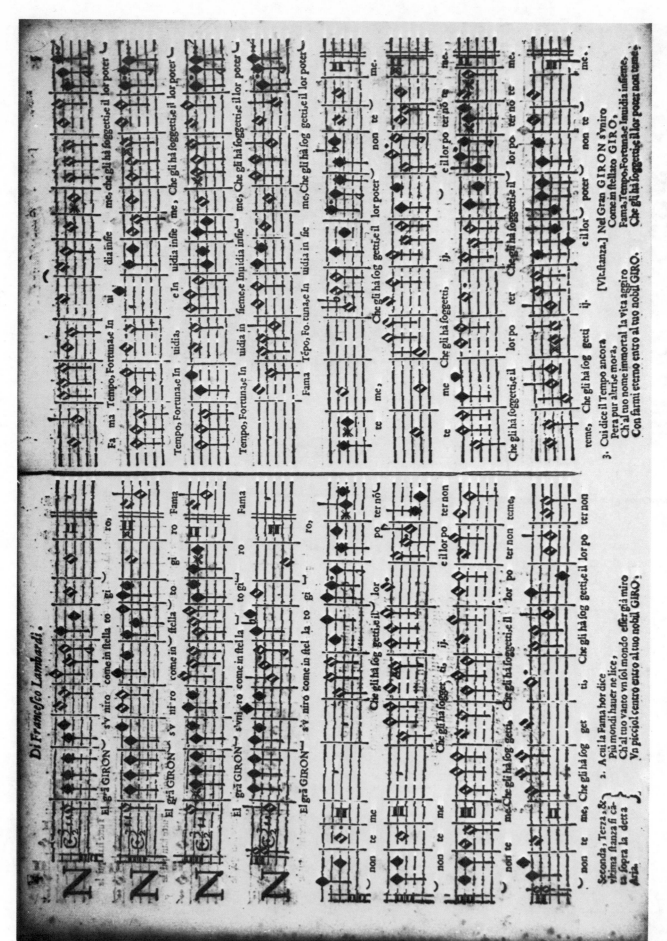

Plate II. *Breve Racconto*, original music for No. [3] by Francesco Lambardi.
(Bibliothèque Nationale, Paris.)

A NEAPOLITAN FESTA A BALLO
"Delizie di Posilipo Boscarecce, e Maritime"

[1. Festa riso]

Pietro Antonio Giramo

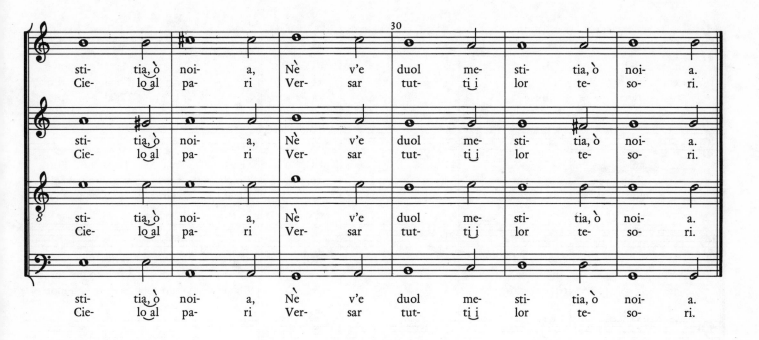

[2. Sebeto ragiona]

Spoken discourse

[3. Nel gran GIRON]

Francesco Lambardi

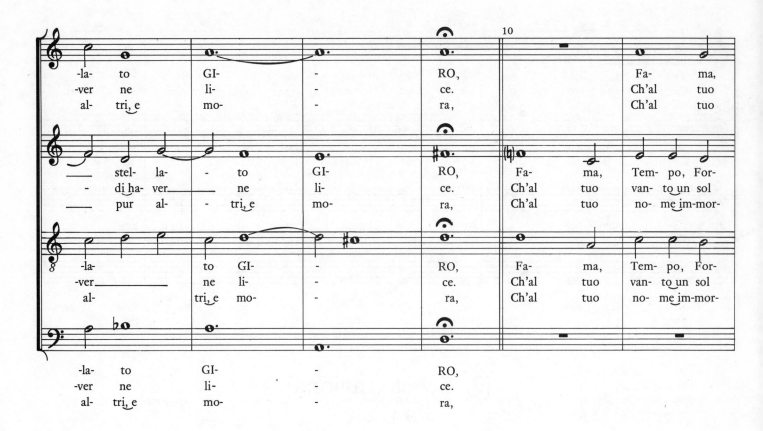

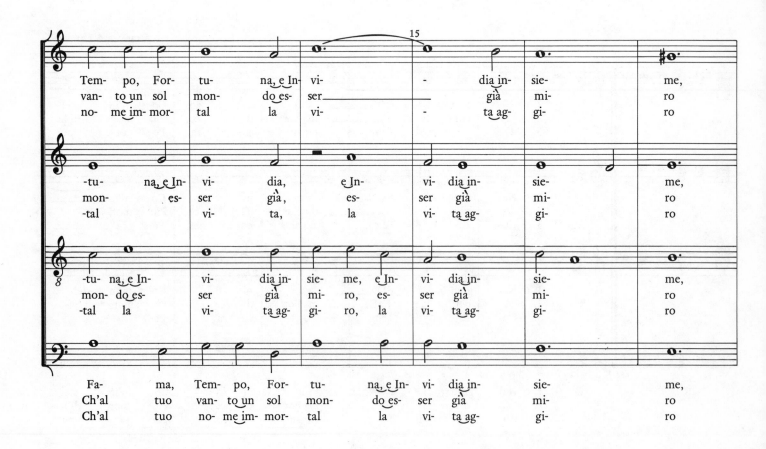

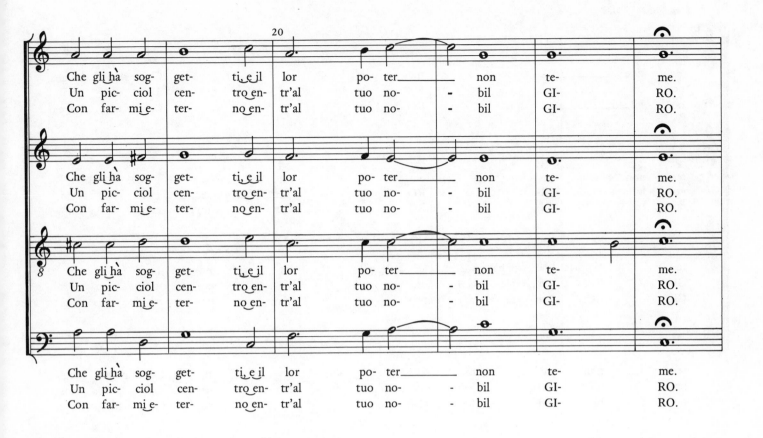

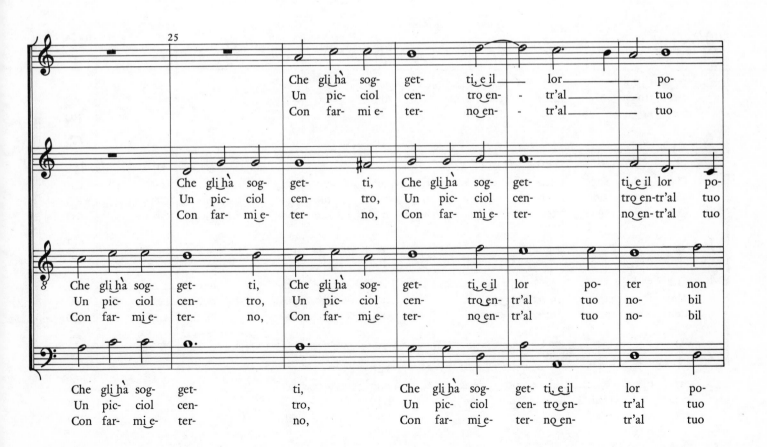

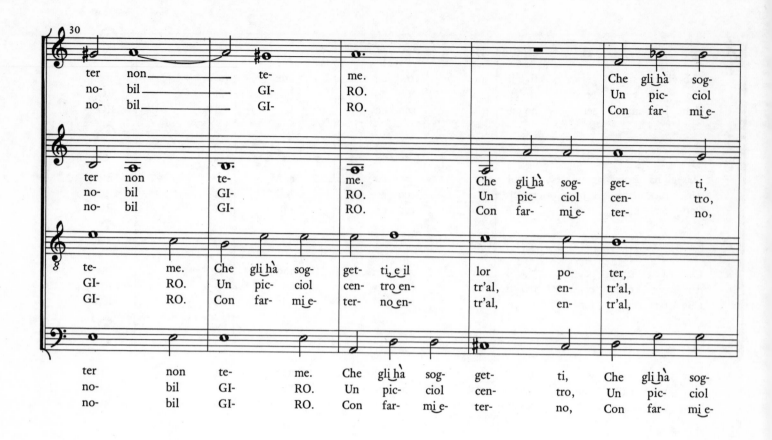

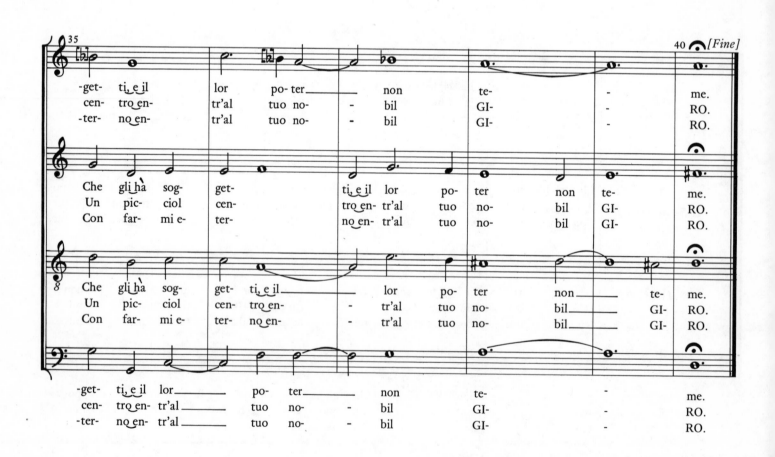

[4.] Aria Prima

Andrea Ansalone

[5.] Arie di tre Sirene

Giovanni Maria Trabaci

Stanza terza, sola

A voi di que- sto gra- to a- me- no

mon- te Di que- sto gen- til

Fiu- me Ca- ro ter- re- no nu-

-me; Ca- ro ter- re- no nu- me;

Stanza quarta a tre

Bel Sol del no- stro Ciel va- go e se- re- no,

E gran Net- tu- no a noi del mar Tir- rhe-

E gran Net- tu- no a noi del mar Tir- rhe-

-no,

del mar Tir- rhe- no,

-no, E gran Net- tu- no a noi del mar Tir- rhe- no,

del mar Tir- rhe- no, del mar Tir- rhe- no,

16

Ultima stanza della tre Sirene, a tre voci

[6. Entrance of Pan]

No music in source

[7.] Il suono della scesa de'Pastori dal monte su'l ponte sonato da quaranta vary istromenti detta la Mendozza

Andrea Ansalone

[8. Exit of Pan]

No music in source

[9. Aria de Venere]

Gio. Maria Trabaci

[sic]

Si sona

1. Don-   ne mie ca-   re Che n'ac-   qui-
2. Qual_____   de' vo-str'oc-chi Fe-ri₋o   be-
3. Tal_____   hog-gi₋i-nan-zi De'i lor   bei
4. A_____   voi gl'in-vi-   o,   Ch'a   di-   let-

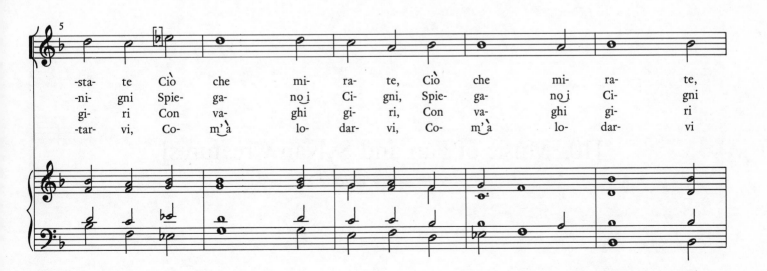

-sta-   te Ciò   che   mi-   ra-   te, Ciò   che   mi-   ra-   te,
-ni-gni Spie-   ga-   no₋i Ci-gni, Spie-   ga-   no₋i Ci-gni
gi-ri Con   va-   ghi gi-ri, Con   va-   ghi gi-ri
-tar-vi, Co-   m'a   lo-   dar-   vi, Co-   m'a   lo-   dar-vi

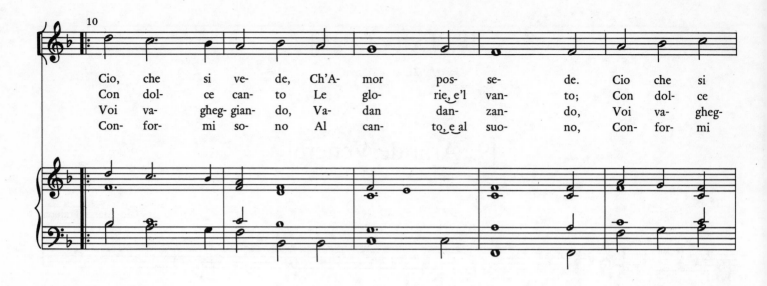

Cio, che si ve- de, Ch'A- mor pos- rie se- de. Cio che si
Con dol- ce can- to Le glo- rie, e'l van- to; Con dol- ce
Voi va- gheg- gian- do, Va- dan dan- zan- do, Voi va- gheg- mi
Con for- mi so- no Al can- to, e al suo- no, Con for- mi

ve- de, Ch'A- mor pos- rie se- de, Ch'A- mor_____ pos se- de.
can- to, Le glo- rie, e'l van- to; Le glo- rie, e'l van- to;
-gian- do, Va- dan dan- zan- do, Va- dan_____ dan- zan- do.
so- no Al can- to, e al suo- no, Al can- to, e al suo- no.

[10. Music of Pan and Sylvan Creatures]

No music in source

[11.] Aria Seconda

Andrea Ansalone

[12.] Suono del Ballo de Cigni
sonato da violini

Giacomo Spiardo

[13. Lenguas son]

Francesco Lambardi

Len- guas son de- ste mon- te pie- dras, y plan- tas, Que al- a-

Len- guas son de- ste mon- te pie- dras, y plan- tas, Que al-a-

Len- guas son de- ste mon- te pie- dras, y plan- tas, Que al-a-

Len- guas son de- ste mon- te pie- dras, y plan- tas, Que al-a-

-ban- do her-mo- su- ras mi- la- - gros can- tan.

-ban- do her-mo- su- ras mi- - la- - gros can- tan.

-ban- do her-mo- su- ras mi- la- - gros can- tan.

-ban- do her-mo- su- ras - mi- la- - gros can- tan.

Len- guas son de- stas pla- - yas, on-

Len- guas son de- stas pla- - yas, on- das y flo- res, y

Len- guas son de- stas pla- - yas, Len- guas son de- stas

Len- guas son, Len- guas son de- stas

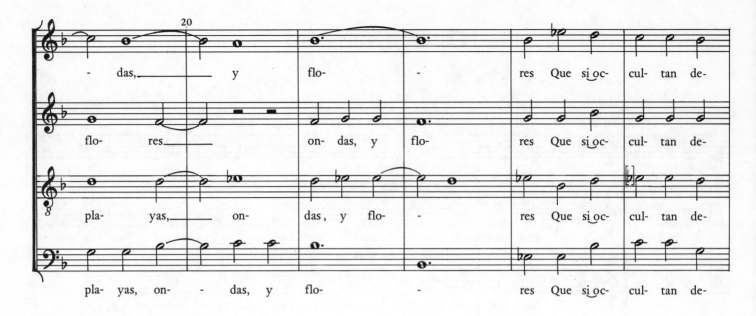

-das,_____ y flo - res Que si oc- cul- tan de-
flo - res_____ on- das, y flo - res Que si oc- cul- tan de-
pla- yas,_____ on - das, y flo - res Que si oc- cul- tan de-
pla- yas, on - das, y flo - res Que si oc- cul- tan de-

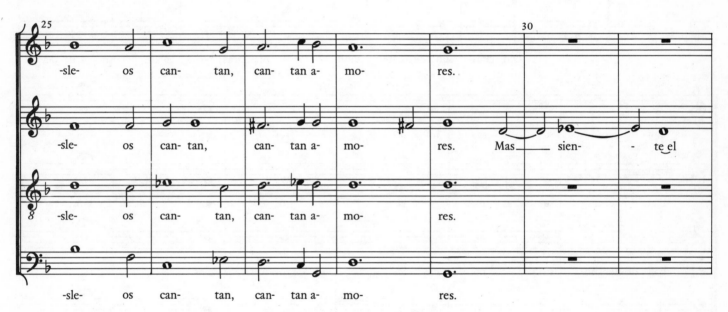

-sle- os can- tan, can- tan a- mo- res.
-sle- os can- tan, can- tan a- mo- res. Mas_____ sien - te el
-sle- os can- tan, can- tan a- mo- res.
-sle- os can- tan, can- tan a- mo- res.

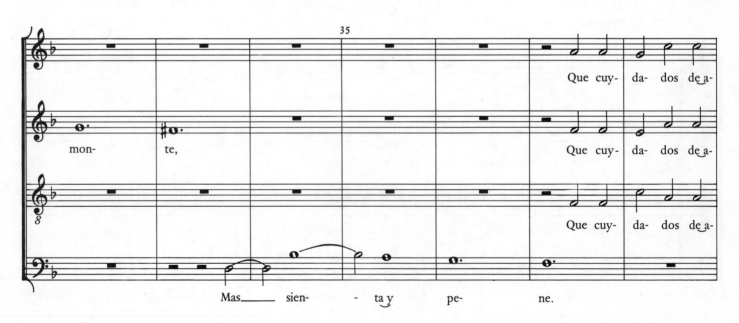

Que cuy- da- dos de a-
mon- te, Que cuy- da- dos de a-
Que cuy- da- dos de a-
Mas_____ sien- ta y pe- ne.

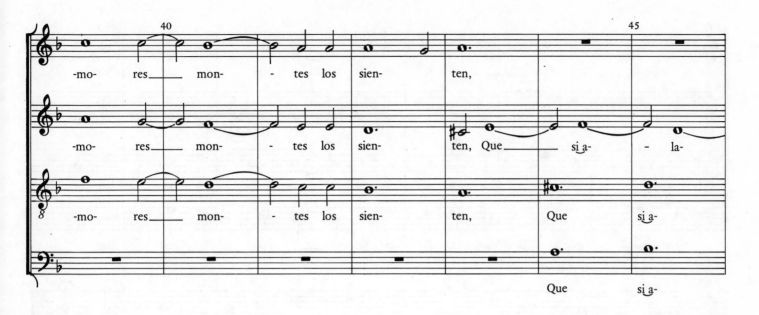

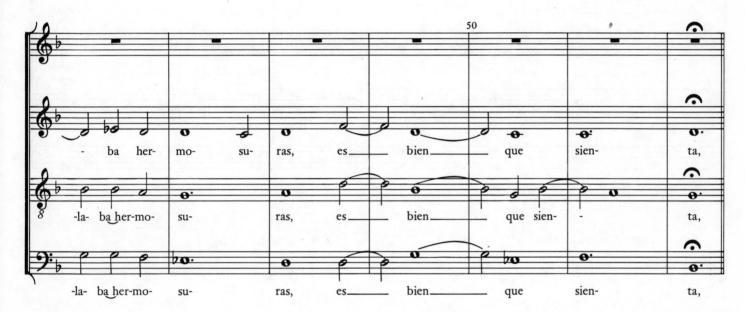

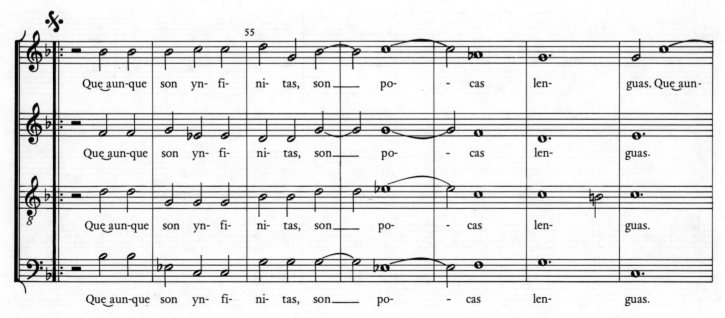

Primera Copla dice solo el Alto

Copla dice solo el Basso

Ba- ya, E- na- ria, y Cu- ma Es- me- ral- das, y___ Za- fi-

-ros En o- las co- - mo en su- spi- ros Os___ pre-

-sen- - tan; Mas se a- fren- tan, Que al cul- to de tal Dey-

-dad To- do pier- de su vel- dad; Pues___ si os a- la- ban con- fie- san,

[D.S.]

[D.S.]

[14.] Suono del Ballo de'Selvaggi, e delle Simie, sonato da istromenti di fiato

Giacomo Spiardo

[15. Dance of Pan and Venus]

No music in source

[16.] Cupido solo dice

Francesco Lambardi

1. Da que- st'ac- que, Da cui nac- que Mia gran
2. A voi sor- go, E vi por- go Que- ste
3. In lor scoc- chi Da, vo- str'oc- chi Sol quel
4. Dun- que lie- te Ri- ce- ve- te Que- sti a-

Si sona

ma- dre, e_____ chia- ra De- a, Ci- te- re - a;
schie- re, e_____ que- sti a- man- ti Fe- steg- gian - ti,
stral, la_____ cui fe- ri- ta Gli da vi - ta,
-man- ti, a _____ la cui fe- de Fia mer- ce - de

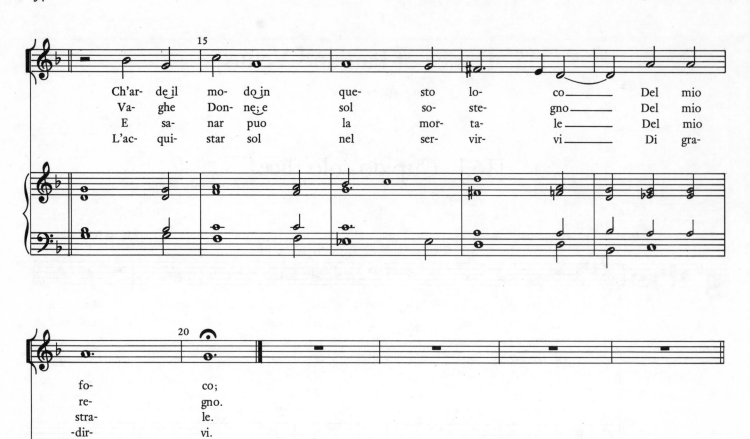

Ch'ar- de il mo- do in que- sto lo- co———— Del mio
Va- ghe Don- ne; e sol so- ste- gno———— Del mio
E sa- nar puo la mor- ta- le———— Del mio
L'ac- qui- star sol nel ser- vir- vi———— Di gra-

fo- co;
re- gno.
stra- le.
-dir- vi.

Ritornello [to be played between each stanza]

[17.] Aria Terza

Andrea Ansalone

SELECTED INSTRUMENTAL ENSEMBLE PIECES
from Naples Conservatory MS 4.6.3.

[1.] Sinfonia antica*

*"Sonata antica" written in alto and bass parts

Seconda partita

Terza partita

[2.] Gagliarda Prima

[3.]   Gagliarda Seconda

[Giovanni da Macque]

[4.] Gagliarda Terza

[5.] Gagliarda Quarta

[6.] Gagliarda Quinta

[7.] Gagliarda Sesta

[Giovanni Maria Trabaci]

*e in ms.

[8.] Gagliarda Settima

[9.] Gagliarda Ottava

[10.] Gagliarda Nona

[Giovanni Maria Trabaci]

[11. Gagliarda]

P[rincip]e di Venosa
[Don Carlo Gesualdo]

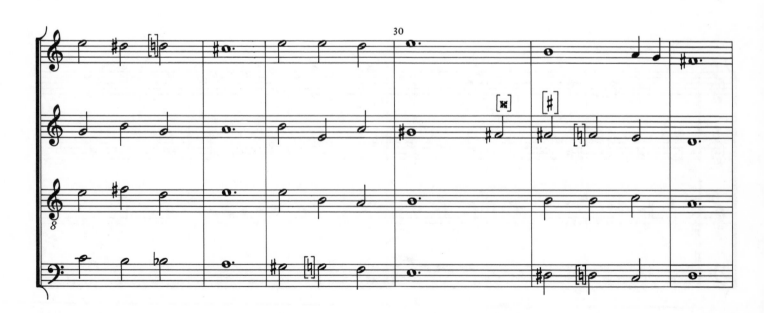

[12.] Gagliarda Falsa

Don Giovanni Maria Sabini

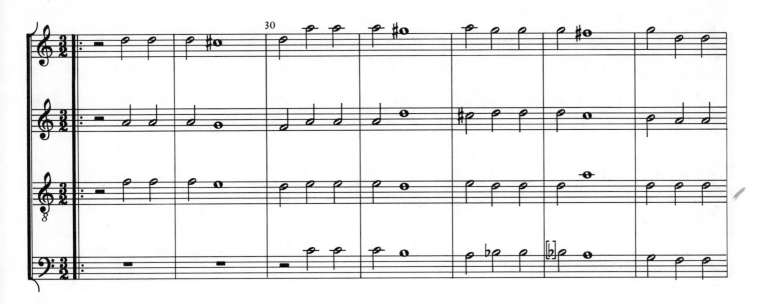

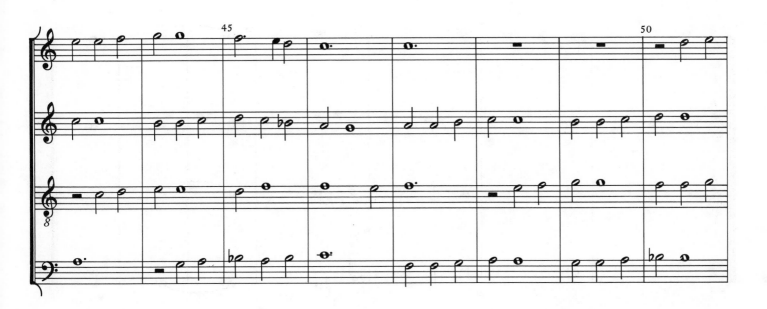

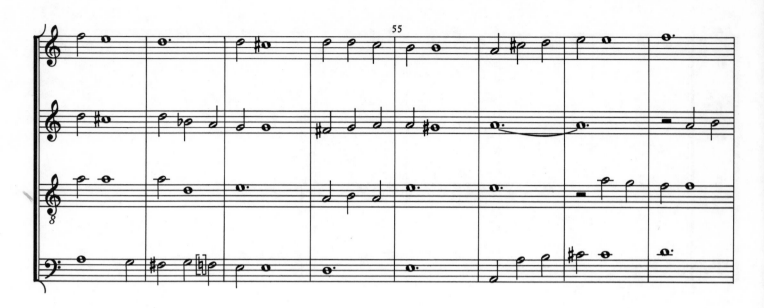

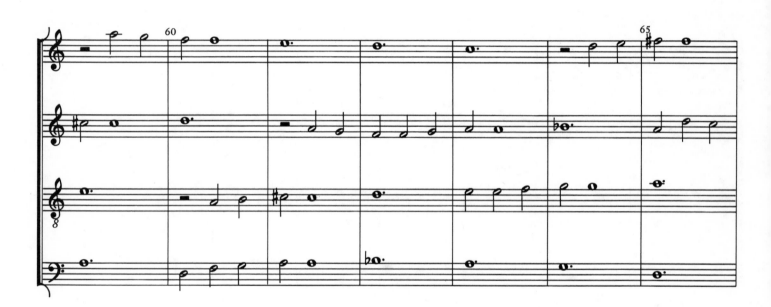

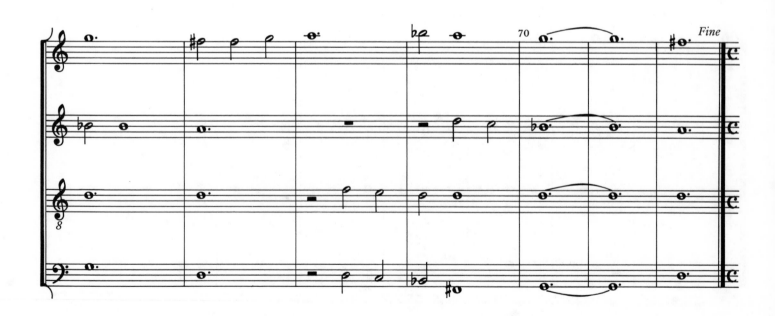

Si replica

[13.] Spagnoletta

Hettorre della Marra

[2nd. time]

[2nd. time]

[2nd. time]

[14.] Gagliarda

[15.] Gagliarda

[?] Arpa

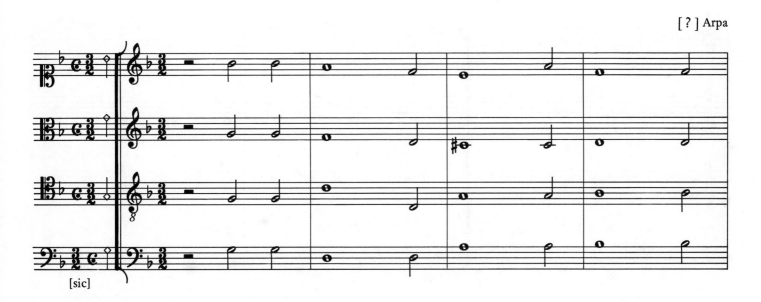

[sic]

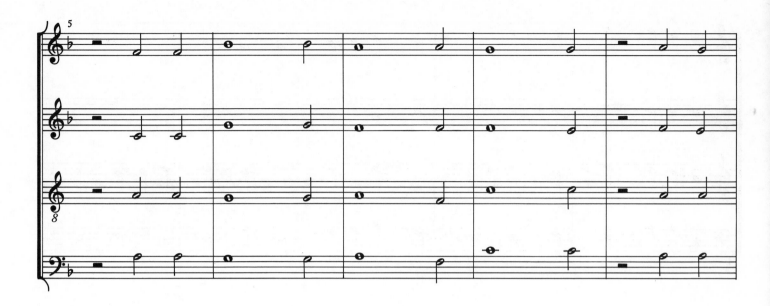

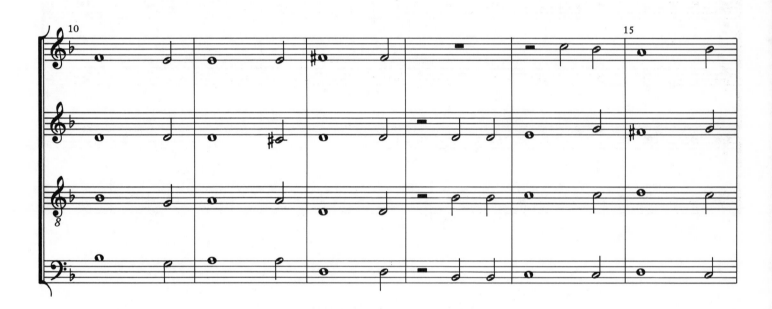

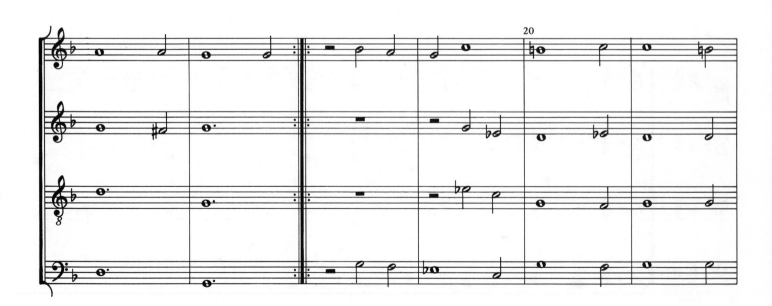

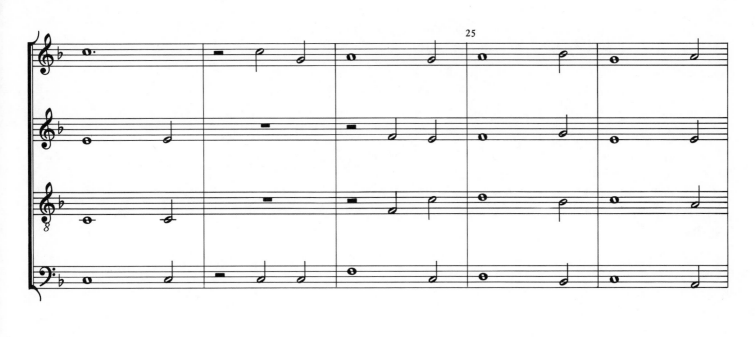

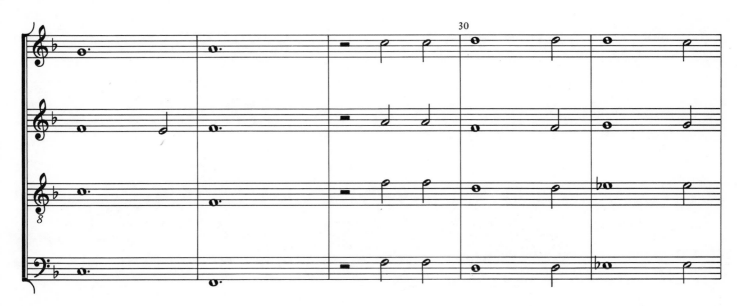

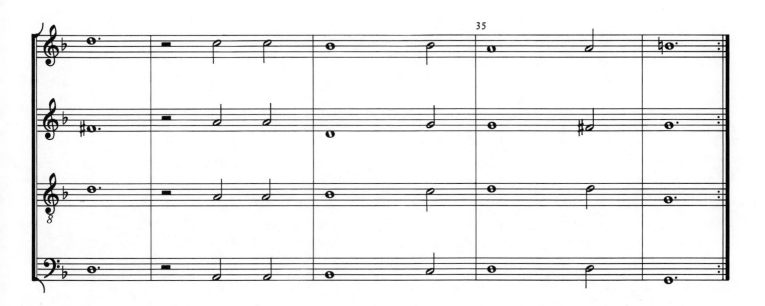